Danger in the
Deep Blue Sea

★ BOOKS IN THIS SERIES ★

TROUBLE AT TRIDENT ACADEMY: BOOK 1

BATTLE OF THE BEST FRIENDS: BOOK 2

A WHALE OF A TALE: BOOK 3

DANGER IN THE DEEP BLUE SEA: BOOK 4

THE LOST PRINCESS: BOOK 5

THE SECRET SEA HORSE: BOOK 6

DREAM OF THE BLUE TURTLE: BOOK 7

TREASURE IN TRIDENT CITY: BOOK 8

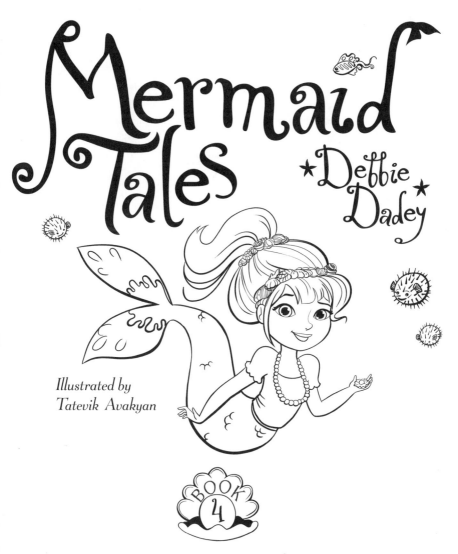

Mermaid Tales

Debbie Dadey

Illustrated by
Tatevik Avakyan

BOOK 4

Danger in the Deep Blue Sea

ALADDIN

NEW YORK   LONDON   TORONTO   SYDNEY   NEW DELHI

ABDO
Spotlight

ABDOPUBLISHING.COM

Reinforced library bound edition published in 2015 by Spotlight, a division of ABDO, PO Box 398166, Minneapolis, Minnesota 55439. Spotlight produces high-quality reinforced library bound editions for schools and libraries. Published by agreement with Aladdin.

Printed in the United States of America, North Mankato, Minnesota.
112014
012015

 THIS BOOK CONTAINS RECYCLED MATERIALS

ALADDIN

An imprint of Simon & Schuster Children's Publishing Division
1230 Avenue of the Americas, New York, NY 10020
First Aladdin paperback edition January 2013
Text copyright © 2013 by Debbie Dadey
Illustrations copyright © 2013 by Tatevik Avakyan
All rights reserved, including the right of reproduction in whole or in part in any form.
ALADDIN is a trademark of Simon & Schuster, Inc., and related logo is a registered trademark of Simon & Schuster, Inc.

LIBRARY OF CONGRESS CATALOGING-IN-PUBLICATION DATA

This book was previously cataloged with the following information:

Dadey, Debby.
 Danger in the deep blue sea / Debby Dadey ; illustrated by Tatevik Avakyan.
 p. cm. (Mermaid tales ; bk. 4)
Summary: A shark has been spotted in Trident City! Pearl Swamp is so scared, she needs a shark Guard to escort her to and from school. She doesn't trust anyone who likes these terrifying creatures, especially Kiki Coral, who isn't nearly as frightened as Pearl. And to make matters worse, Pearl accuses Kiki of stealing her precious pearl necklace! Will the sharks destroy the peace of their sparking city? Or will the mergirls have to swim in dangerous deep-sea waters?
1. Mermaids--Juvenile fiction. 2. Friendship--Juvenile fiction. I. Avakyan, Tatevik, 1983- ill.
[Fic]--dc23
PZ7.D128 Dan 2013
                          2012950425

978-1-61479-325-0 (reinforced library bound edition)

Spotlight

A Division of ABDO
abdopublishing.com

To Blakely Fow.
May your life be filled with much joy.

★ ★ ★ ★

Acknowledgments

Thanks to my Pennsylvania critique group for the awesome support: Wendy Greenley, Kathe Everitt, Joanne Alburger, and Tamara Gureghian.

Cast of Characters

Shelly

Echo

Kiki

Pearl

Rocky

Contents

1   LATE-BREAKING NEWS!   1

2   SHARK PATROL   6

3   SKELETON   13

4   MISSING   20

5   HEADMASTER HERMIT   28

6   STINKY OLD THING   36

7   MOVING DAY   44

8   SHARK!   57

9   TRAPPED   62

10 SURPRISE   69

    CLASS REPORTS   77

    THE MERMAID TALES SONG   83

    AUTHOR'S NOTE   85

    GLOSSARY   87

Late-Breaking News!

"OH MY NEPTUNE!" PEARL Swamp shrieked as she swam into the huge front hallway of Trident Academy. "Did you see the newspaper this morning?"

Wanda Slug, Pearl's good friend, shook her head. "No, I didn't," she said. "I had

to finish my homework before school."
The two mergirls floated out of the way
of some fourth-grade merboys who zoomed
past them.

Trident Academy was a prestigious
school in Trident City. Third-grade

through tenth-grade merkids came from all over the ocean to study in the enormous clamshell. The front hall alone was big enough for a humpback whale to take a nap in.

Pearl's blond hair and long strand of pearls swirled in the water as merstudents rushed around her to get to their classrooms. "My dad made me read the front page," she told Wanda. "You'll never believe it! There have been shark sightings in Trident City!"

"What?" Wanda gasped. "Are you kidding? That's terrible." Sharks were the number one danger to the merpeople community.

Pearl's green eyes widened. "I'm serious.

I couldn't even swim here by myself. My father hired a Shark Patrol Guard to escort me to and from school."

Wanda shuddered. "I'm glad I live in the Trident Academy dorm. I wouldn't want to be swimming home with a shark on my tail." Both girls looked at their own mertails and wiggled them gently. Neither girl noticed that the front hall was almost empty of merstudents.

Pearl slapped her gold tail on the shell floor and folded her arms across her chest. "This is ridiculous. What's wrong with this place? Can't they keep scary sharks from chasing people? Something should be done."

"Yeah, but what can we do?" Wanda said. "We're just third graders."

Pearl twisted her necklace in her fingers. "I hate being scared and I hate having a Shark Guard. My dad might not even let me go to Tail Flippers practice if things get worse!"

"No!" Wanda gasped. Tail Flippers was the school's dance and gymnastics team.

Pearl sighed. "I don't know what I'm going to do, but I'm going to do something. I refuse to let sharks ruin my life."

"Uh-oh," Wanda said, finally noticing the empty hall. "We'd better get to class or *Mrs. Karp* will ruin our lives!"

Shark Patrol

PEARL AND WANDA MADE IT to class just as the conch shell sounded. Pearl swam up to her teacher's desk. "Mrs. Karp, did you hear the terrible news?" she asked. "A shark has been spotted in Trident City! Can't something be done?"

Echo Reef, one of the third graders, raised her hand. "Is it true?" she said in a trembling voice.

"My grandfather saw it in the paper," Shelly Siren said. She nervously flicked her blue tail.

"Are we in danger here at Trident Academy?" Kiki Coral asked. She was the smallest mergirl in the third grade.

The twenty merstudents looked to their teacher for an answer. Mrs. Karp ran a hand through her green hair. "I am sure the Shark Patrol is doing everything in their power to protect us. We can't panic," she said.

"But what if it's not *enough*?" Pearl cried. The thought of sharks swimming near the school made her feel sick.

"Remember the first rule of shark safety and you should be fine," Mrs. Karp said, pointing to the Shark Safety Rules chart that hung from a seaweed curtain. "Shelly, please read rule number one."

SHARK SAFETY RULES

1. NEVER SWIM ALONE
2. BE ALERT

Shelly cleared her throat and said in a shaky voice, "NEVER SWIM ALONE." Pearl sniffed. Why did Mrs. Karp always call on Shelly? Was it just because her grandfather was a famous human expert? Pearl knew she could read just as well as Shelly.

Rocky Ridge, one of the merboys in class, piped up, "Don't cry, Pearl. A shark wouldn't want to bite you. You're more sour than sweet."

"You're the only sour one around here," Pearl said, sticking her tongue out at him. "I bet you're just as scared as I am!"

"Class, please pass your homework in," Mrs. Karp instructed, trying to change the subject.

Their schoolwork was done on small pieces of seaweed and written with orange sea pens and octopus ink. All around the classroom the merkids handed seaweed to the merstudent in front of them. Everyone except Rocky, who tapped his thumbs on his rock desk and whistled a shark song. Several mergirls whispered nervously about the shark.

"Mrs. Karp? Should we be worried?" Kiki asked.

Mrs. Karp looked at the frightened faces of the mergirls and merboys. She didn't lie to her merstudents. "Of course, when you live in the ocean, as we do, you must always be on the lookout for dangerous creatures who want to eat you. It's part of the ocean life cycle."

"That's just disgusting," Pearl said. "I don't want to be part of a life cycle."

"You mean if we lived on land, we wouldn't have to worry about sharks?" Echo asked. The whole class knew how much Echo loved everything about humans. She hoped to get the chance to see one someday.

"Only if you went into the water," Mrs. Karp said. "That's the one advantage humans have over us."

"Maybe I want to be human, then," Pearl snapped.

The entire class gasped. Merpeople were not supposed to speak like that. There was an ancient legend about a beautiful mer-maid who had turned into a human. No one knew what had happened to her, but there were creepy stories about a witch chasing her. Merkids told scary tales about it late at night during sleepover parties.

"Humans can't even breathe under-water!" Rocky said, breaking the tension.

"That's right," Kiki agreed. "I heard they even drink water!"

Everyone in the class laughed at the silliness of that idea. Drinking water! Why would anyone do that?

3

Skeleton

URING LUNCH PEARL AND Wanda sat together in the cafeteria with other mergirls from their class. As usual, merkids of all ages talked and ate their lunches at polished granite tables decorated with the gold Trident Academy logo. On special days, all the merstudents would wear different colored sashes to show which grade they were in, but today only a few bothered.

"They're doing it again," Wanda said, pointing to the front of the lunchroom, where Shelly, Echo, and Kiki stood in front of Mr. Fangtooth, the cafeteria worker.

"He's such a grump," Pearl said, pushing her black-lip oyster and sablefish stew around in its shell bowl. "They'll never be able to cheer him up. Why do they always try so hard to make him laugh? Who cares if he smiles or if he's happy?"

Still, Pearl and Wanda watched as Kiki, Echo, and Shelly wiggled seaweed under their noses. Mr. Fangtooth shook his head and scraped their crab casserole crumbs into the hagfish disposal. He didn't crack a small smile or a big grin. The three mergirls sighed and swam back to their table in the corner.

"I can't even enjoy my favorite dish," Pearl complained. "All this talk of sharks has me too upset."

"At least *you* don't have to sleep with a shark," Wanda whined. All the mergirls at their table stopped eating and stared at her.

"*What* are you talking about?" asked Pearl.

Wanda nodded toward Kiki. "You know

that Kiki is my roommate. But her bed isn't a bed at all, it's a huge skeleton. It reminds me of a shark, but it's actually a killer whale skeleton. It's disgusting. It gives me nightmares!"

"That's awful," Wanda's friend Morgan whispered.

Wanda yawned. "I'm having trouble sleeping, and I'm too tired to do my school-work."

Pearl could see the huge, dark circles under Wanda's eyes. Pearl had been jealous of Wanda because she got to live in the school dormitory since her home was so far away. But now Pearl was glad she lived close to school, even if she did have to have a Shark Guard. Who knew what kind of roommate she'd be stuck with?

The girls at the table shuddered, but most of them continued eating their long-horn cowfish daily special. Pearl didn't eat. She couldn't eat. She was too horrified.

"That's terrible," Pearl said.

"That's not the worst of it. I'm hardly ever in my room," Wanda explained. "I study in the library because that awful skeleton is so creepy. I feel like, if I turn my back, it's going to eat me!"

The other mergirls laughed, but not Pearl. She knew a skeleton couldn't eat anyone. But when she was six years old, she had seen a shark skeleton in the front hallway of the Conservatory for the Pres-ervation of Sea Horses and Swordfish.

For weeks afterward she'd been so scared she'd needed a jellyfish nightlight to fall asleep.

"I want to see it," Pearl said.

Wanda shrugged. "I'll take you there after school."

Pearl shook her head. "I want to see that skeleton *right now*."

"We can't," Wanda explained. "We're not allowed to go to our dorm rooms during school. That's the rule."

Pearl rolled her eyes. "Rules are for people who don't know better. Let's go."

FIVE MINUTES LATER, PEARL STOOD IN front of Kiki's enormous killer whale skeleton. Each rib was as big as Pearl's arm.

★ 18 ★

The nest of gray heron feathers inside the skeleton didn't make it any less dreadful.

"See?" Wanda said. "I told you it was hideous."

Pearl didn't argue. Memories of the skeleton in the Conservatory for the Preservation of Sea Horses and Swordfish came flooding back.

"You shouldn't have to be scared all the time," she told Wanda. "I'm going to help you. I may not be able to do anything about the sharks in Trident City, but this is something I can fix. Just you wait and see."

Missing

SWEET SEAWEED!" PEARL SNAPPED
to her Shark Guard. "This is so
embarrassing. What if someone
sees you?"

The Shark Guard shrugged. He looked
huge next to Pearl. "Just doing my job,

miss." Pearl groaned and floated off toward Tail Flippers practice. It was after school and MerPark was quickly filling up with merkids practicing Shell Wars, a game where a small shell is hit into a treasure chest guarded by an octopus. Pearl saw Rocky and Shelly smacking a shell back and forth.

Tail Flippers practice was held just past the Shell Wars field. Pearl crossed her fingers that no one would notice the big hulk following her. She wasn't so lucky.

"Hey, Pearl," Rocky yelled. "Who is your babysitter?" He waved his long whale bone Shell Wars stick at her

"Don't you worry about it. Just go play

your nasty Shell Wars." Pearl swam off as quickly as she could, but she could still hear Rocky's teasing.

"Pearl has a babysitter. Pearl has a babysitter."

"That Rocky is such a pain," Pearl complained to Echo and the other mergirls at Tail Flippers. Luckily, she had made it to practice before Coach Barnacle. He was very strict about team members being on time.

Echo giggled. "I think Rocky is kind of cute, though. Goofy, but cute."

The other girls laughed and started stretching their tails. Pearl pulled off her perfectly matched, white pearl necklace and gently placed it on a rock near the practice field. Her Shark Guard floated over to a nearby merstatue and leaned against it.

"Your necklace is one of the prettiest I've ever seen," Kiki said, swimming up beside Pearl. Pearl ignored her compliment.

"Aren't you Wanda's roommate?" Pearl asked as she looked Kiki—and her unusual purple tail—up and down. A few other mergirls floated onto the field.

Kiki nodded. Her long black hair swirled around her. "Wanda was the first person I met when I came here," Kiki said with a smile.

"Well, you're not a very nice roommate. It's terrible that you make Wanda sleep with a stinky old shark carcass," Pearl growled.

★ 23 ★

Instantly, Kiki's smile disappeared. "It's a killer whale, not a shark."

"It's still disgusting!" Then Pearl asked her, "Why are you here, anyway? You aren't a Tail Flipper. You didn't even try out."

Shaking her head, Kiki replied, "I'm allowed to be here. I came to watch Echo. She's my close friend."

Pearl frowned. "I bet Echo doesn't even know you sleep in a horror chamber. I think I'll tell her how creepy it is!"

Kiki was too shocked to answer.

Just then Coach Barnacle swam onto

the kelp field. "Okay, merladies," Coach announced. "Let's get to practicing."

Kiki sped off the field toward the Trident Academy dormitory. She didn't stay to watch Echo or the Tail Flippers.

Echo called out, "Let's catch up later, Kiki."

"Good riddance," Pearl said.

"Quiet now, Pearl," Coach Barnacle said. "Please show me your backflip." Nobody said no to Coach Barnacle. He wasn't an ordinary merman. He was a Centauro-triton. His tail looked like a dolphin's, and he had a fin running along the back of it.

The team worked on their backflips and round-off front handsprings. Pearl was dizzy as Coach Barnacle taught them their very first complete Tail Flippers routine. It was hard to listen to the music he hummed and remember when to flip and when to spring. When they finished, Echo slumped to the ocean floor. "That was exhausting," she said.

"You said it," Pearl agreed. "I hope Coach doesn't work us that hard every time!"

Pearl was so tired, she forgot to tell Echo about Kiki's skeleton.

Echo nodded. "I bet my tail will be sore tomorrow!"

"No kidding," Pearl said, rubbing her own golden tail. As she looked around MerPark, she noticed her Shark Guard

taking a nap next to a statue. Pearl won-
dered if she should tell her father about her
guard sleeping on the job. She swam slowly
over to the rock where she'd left her pearl
necklace. She was so worn out she didn't
know if she'd have the strength to lift it
over her head. But when she reached the
rock, she made a surprising discovery.

"My necklace!" Pearl screamed. "It's
gone! Someone has stolen my necklace!"

Headmaster Hermit

SHE TOOK IT!" PEARL POINTED her finger across Headmaster Hermit's large office at Kiki.

Kiki slid down in her polished marble chair and whispered, "No, I didn't, Headmaster. I promise. I didn't touch Pearl's necklace."

Headmaster Hermit tapped his chin with his long black tail. "Perhaps you forgot and left your necklace at home, Pearl. After all, pearls are not appropriate jewelry for merstudents at school."

The headmaster frowned at Pearl, but it didn't stop her from leaping up from her chair. "I know I wore it, sir. You can even ask my Shark Guard if he saw it. Kiki admired my necklace when I put it on the rock. I'm sure she has my pearls!"

Kiki spoke softly. "I did tell Pearl it was pretty, but I didn't take it. I would never steal anything!"

"I am sure you wouldn't," the headmaster stated. "But in light of the problem, perhaps we should check all of the rooms.

We cannot have this kind of behavior at Trident Academy."

"If you look in Kiki's room first, you'll find it," Pearl blurted. "She also has a horrible shark in there. I bet that's against the rules. Just like stealing!"

"A *shark*!" Headmaster Hermit shouted

and slapped his marble desk with his tail. "What is going on here? Don't we have enough trouble without joking about sharks in dorm rooms! That is not funny, Miss Swamp!"

Kiki held up a hand in explanation. "A skeleton, sir! It's a killer whale skeleton, not a shark."

Pearl sniffed. "It looks like a shark."

The headmaster let out a deep breath and said, "Well, let's go take a look at this room, if you don't mind, Miss Coral. We won't do it without your consent."

Kiki sat up straight. "I have nothing to hide."

"Come this way, girls," Headmaster Hermit said as he floated out the door.

Pearl swam behind him, determined to find her necklace. Kiki followed with her head down, and bumped into Echo and Shelly, who were waiting outside the headmaster's office. Shelly still carried her whale bone stick from Shell Wars practice.

Echo floated over to Pearl. "What happened?" she asked as the headmaster swam ahead toward the girls' dorm.

Shelly put her hand on Kiki's shoulder. "Are you all right?" Shelly asked.

"Don't worry. I'm fine," Kiki said.

"I'm not fine," Pearl said. "*She* stole my necklace."

Shelly scrunched up her nose at Pearl. "Kiki wouldn't do that!"

Echo looked from Pearl to Kiki and said, "You didn't, did you, Kiki?"

A tiny tear slid down the small mergirl's cheek. "Do you really think I would steal Pearl's necklace?"

"If you didn't steal it, then where is it?" Pearl demanded.

"Ladies," Headmaster Hermit called to the girls. "Come along now. Let's proceed."

The head of Trident Academy enlisted Mrs. Karp's help to look through the dorm rooms one by one. At last they came to Kiki and Wanda's room and carefully searched it together.

Pearl stood by, her arms across her chest. Shelly and Echo each had a hand on Kiki's back. Finally the headmaster shook his head.

"Pearl, you are mistaken. There is no pearl necklace in this area. In fact, the only problem here is that Kiki has a terribly messy roommate."

Shelly giggled and whispered to Echo, "Wanda is Kiki's roommate. Kiki is as neat as a cowrie shell."

Pearl wasn't happy. "Then where is my

necklace?" she asked in a sharp voice.

"Young merlady!" Headmaster Hermit roared. "You are addressing the headmaster of Trident Academy. There is no excusing your rude tone!"

Pearl gulped. "I'm sorry, sir. I was just concerned about my pearls."

Mrs. Karp patted Pearl on the shoulder. "We'll ask Mr. Fangtooth to keep an eye out for your jewelry. He knows everything that goes on around here. He'll find it."

Headmaster Hermit, Mrs. Karp, and Pearl floated out of the room.

Pearl turned and looked straight at Kiki.

"You'll be sorry," Pearl hissed. "Just wait and see."

6

Stinky Old Thing

ONCE AGAIN, JUST LIKE THE morning before, Pearl's Shark Guard escorted her to the front entrance of Trident Academy. She had come early so Rocky wouldn't tease her again.

But Wanda zoomed over to Pearl, upset and screaming.

"*What* did you do?" Wanda said loudly. The morning light shone on the beautifully carved ceiling, but neither mergirl paid any attention to it or anything else in the vast hall.

Pearl flashed her green eyes and smiled. "I told you I was going to help. I got my mom to petition the school so that no one can have skeletons in their shared dorm rooms."

"Petition? What's that?" Wanda asked.

"It's where you complain about something on a piece of seaweed and get other people to agree," Pearl explained. "My mom got all the merladies in her social club to sign it at our house last night. That silly Headmaster Hermit will have to make Kiki move out. And as soon as this shark scare is over, my mom is going to have a meeting with him about my pearls."

"But what about Kiki? What will happen to her?" Wanda said.

Pearl shrugged. "She'll have to throw away that stinky old skeleton. I bet it's full of germs. That's if she doesn't get kicked out of school. Then she can move back with her seventeen brothers."

Wanda put her hand to her mouth. "But it's her bed. She's going to hate me now! Maybe there's another way."

"Why do you care?" Pearl said. "I did

what you wanted. I got rid of the skeleton so you can sleep and study. Don't be so ungrateful."

"Pearl, I can't believe you. You don't understand anything," Wanda cried, and rushed out of the front hall toward the dormitories.

Pearl shouted after her, "Where are you going? We don't want to be late for class!"

But Wanda didn't answer. Pearl sighed and shook her head. "She didn't even thank me." Still, Pearl was curious to see what Wanda was going to do, so she caught up to her.

Wanda and Pearl found Kiki moving the huge killer whale skeleton out of her room. The bed's gray heron feathers floated all over the hallway. Kiki pulled and tugged with all her might. Echo and Shelly pushed the back, trying to get the big skeleton out of the dorm room. They stopped when they saw Wanda and Pearl.

Wanda put her hand on Kiki's shoulder. "I'm so sorry," Wanda told her. "I didn't know Pearl was going to do this."

Pearl smoothed back her blond hair.

"I don't know what you are complaining about, Wanda. You wanted the skeleton gone. I made it happen."

"It's all right, Wanda," Kiki said. "I know not everyone likes killer whales."

Echo spoke directly to Pearl. "I hate killer whales. And I hate skeletons. But I would never be this mean to Kiki!"

Grabbing one side of the skeleton,

Wanda announced, "Well, at least I can help." Together, the four girls pulled the killer whale into the hallway.

"I don't know how you can stand up for someone who steals necklaces from innocent merpeople!" Pearl shouted.

Wanda looked at Pearl and said, "I know that Headmaster Hermit didn't find your pearls in our room."

"That doesn't mean anything," Pearl said. "Kiki could have hidden them somewhere else."

Shelly stopped in her tracks, her red hair streaming behind her. She yelled, "Kiki didn't steal anything!"

"How do you know that?" Pearl answered back. "After all, you've only known Kiki for a few weeks, since school started."

"I just know," Shelly said.

Echo didn't say a word. She stared at Kiki and touched the glittering plankton bow in her own curly black hair.

Pearl turned her pointed nose up in the water and swam down the hallway. She didn't care what Wanda did. Or Echo, or Shelly, or Kiki. As far as Pearl was concerned, they were all horrible, and she hoped they'd get in trouble for being late to school.

She knew she had done the right thing. Why couldn't anyone else see that?

Moving Day

LATER THAT MORNING, AFTER THEIR mermath lesson, Mrs. Karp floated to the front of the classroom. She cleared her throat and said, "I know most of you are still a bit nervous about the shark sightings. So I think this is a good time for us to learn more about these creatures. We will go to the library, and you'll do a short report on the shark of your choice."

Rocky raised his hand. "A dead shark is my favorite kind."

Mrs. Karp raised her green eyebrows. "Please keep in mind that sharks are needed for our ecosystem to function properly. Without sharks to eat weak and diseased fish, our ocean would be weak and diseased as well." Then she asked Rocky, "Would you like me to select a shark for you?"

"No, thank you," Rocky answered quickly. The merstudents lined up swiftly and swam to the merlibrary, one of Pearl's favorite places in the school. She didn't really care about all the stacks of seaweed books, but she loved the mother-of-pearl dome ceiling and the fancy chandeliers salvaged from a sunken ship. Glowing jellyfish lived on the chandeliers and made them really sparkle. It was too bad they had to learn about disgusting sharks. Pearl just wanted to stare at the ceiling.

"Miss Scylla," Echo said, "that's a pretty necklace you're wearing."

Pearl turned to see the librarian's jewelry. It didn't look so great to Pearl. It was made of small yellow pearls. Her own necklace was much nicer. After all, it had once been her grandmother's. But now it was gone, thanks to Kiki.

Miss Scylla smiled. "I wore it specially today because it's made of pearls from the Shark's Bay oyster."

Pearl groaned. Why couldn't everyone stop talking about sharks?

"Here are some Shark's Bay oysters in this display." Miss Scylla pointed to a box containing small grayish shells.

"You mean these weird-looking things made those pretty pearls you're wearing?" Shelly asked.

Miss Scylla nodded. "They form the pearl around a piece of sand that irritates them."

Rocky started spitting on the floor. "Hey, Miss Scylla," he said between spits. "Pearl irritates me. If my spit makes a pearl necklace, do I still have to do my report?"

"You apologize to Pearl right this minute," Miss Scylla said. "That's not the way to talk to a young merlady."

Pearl ignored Rocky when he apologized. She was staring at the yucky-looking clams. Were the ones who made her beautiful necklace just as icky? She felt like crying. Where was her necklace? She was so upset, she perched in a corner and barely did any work.

Later, in the lunchroom, Pearl sat next to Morgan. Pearl bit into her lunch of black-lip oyster and sablefish stew and chewed. For some reason, it didn't taste as good as it usually did. Morgan slurped her red lionfish roast with gray lichen gravy. It didn't look worth four shells to Pearl. "Why is everyone staring at me that way?" Pearl asked.

Morgan shrugged and looked at the rest of the mergirls at their table. They had moved away from Pearl and were frowning at her between bites of lunch. "I think it has to do with you being mean to Kiki," Morgan whispered.

"Mean!" Pearl yelled. "I wasn't mean. I saved Wanda from a lot of sleepless nights! And bad grades. How would you like to have a killer whale stare at you in your room?"

Morgan gulped and scooted away from Pearl. "I—I—I wouldn't like it," Morgan said, shuddering.

Pearl nodded. "Nobody wants to sleep with skeletons," she insisted. "And why isn't anyone mad at Kiki? Don't forget she's the one who took my necklace!"

Morgan ate her lionfish special and didn't look at Pearl.

Pearl was so mad, she pushed her bowl away. "Everyone should be thanking me. Where is Kiki, anyway? She can't turn everyone against me! I want to give her a piece of my mind!" Pearl looked around the cafeteria. Usually Kiki, Shelly, and Echo sat together, but today Pearl didn't see them anywhere.

"I—I—I think Kiki's moving into a new room," Morgan whimpered.

"*What?* I thought the Trident dorms were full," Pearl yelped, and stormed out of the cafeteria.

"Pearl," Morgan called after her, "you'd

better come back or you'll get in trouble."

"Trouble, my tail," Pearl said. She was too steamed to worry about getting in trouble for leaving the cafeteria without permission. The very idea of people being upset with her, when everything was Kiki's fault!

Pearl raced through the watery halls to the dormitory. She couldn't remember when she had ever been this angry.

She saw Echo, Shelly, and Kiki floating into a storage room. Piles of cleaning supplies stood out in the hallway. The horrible skeleton bed loomed beside the supplies.

"Hi, Pearl," Echo said with a wave. "Are you here to help Kiki move?"

Before Pearl could answer, Wanda floated out of her room carrying a small chest with Kiki's name on it. "What are *you* doing?" Pearl asked Wanda. "Are you really helping Kiki after what she did to me? I thought you were a friend."

Wanda stopped in front of Pearl. "I am a friend. I'm Kiki's friend. I'll be *your* friend too, if you let me."

Kiki smiled. "Hi, Pearl. Would you like to see my new room?"

Pearl couldn't believe her ears. She swam to the beaded doorway and peeked inside. Kiki's new room was twice as big as a regular dorm room. Rainbow-colored jellyfish lamps hung from the curved ceiling, and a small waterfall tinkled gently in one corner. One whole side glittered with plankton while another was aglow with a magnificent coral reef.

"Isn't it cool?" Kiki said. "Mrs. Karp found the lamps for me. Echo and Shelly helped me clean the supplies out. There's room for my bed right in the middle."

Pearl shook her head. "You can't live here."

Kiki put her hand on Pearl's arm. "It's all right. I'm not mad at you for making me move out of Wanda's room."

"This isn't fair!" Pearl said with a slap of her gold tail. "You ended up with a much nicer room."

Kiki giggled. "It's funny how things worked out. Of course, I'll miss Wanda.

But now she won't be scared to study. And we can still be friends."

Pearl shook her fist at Echo. "How could you help Kiki? You know she took my necklace!"

Echo frowned. "No, I don't, Pearl. I just don't believe it. Kiki wouldn't do anything like that! I bet you lost it and blamed it on her."

Shelly nodded. "That sounds like something Pearl would do."

"I did not!" Pearl yelled. She felt her face getting red, and she knew she'd better leave quickly before she cried.

She spun around, knocking the carefully stacked cleaning supplies all over the hallway. She didn't stop to pick them up.

She didn't stop at the cafeteria. She didn't even stop at the headmaster's office to ask to go home early.

Pearl had had enough of school. She was going home. She looked around the entrance for her Shark Guard. He was nowhere to be seen. *Well, I'm not going to wait around all day for him,* Pearl thought. She swam out of Trident Academy without a backward glance, totally alone.

Shark!

OW CAN THEY TREAT ME like I'm the bad merguy?" Pearl muttered as she swam past the statues in MerPark. She felt like kicking the marble sculpture of Poseidon. "I was only trying to help Wanda. She's the one who had to sleep with a scary skeleton."

Pearl was so deep in thought she didn't see the big gray-and-white snout sliding up behind her. "And why does Kiki get a great room when she took my necklace? None of this makes any sense! I'm going to tell my mother when I get home. She'll fix this mess."

Suddenly a massive mouth with three thousand razor-sharp teeth opened right in front of Pearl.

"Oh my Neptune!" she screamed. Pearl was so petrified she couldn't move her shimmering tail one bit.

The teeth belonged to a great white shark that was at least twenty feet long. He looked fierce and mean, and Pearl knew she would never get the chance to complain to her mother. She would never get the chance to complain to anyone ever again. She was sure she was about to become this creature's lunch!

But then Pearl saw something that made her mad, so mad she reached out and banged the shark—hard—on the nose. "How dare you!" she shouted.

Surprised and startled, the shark snapped its jaws shut and backed away. But Pearl wasn't done. She wanted what was in the shark's mouth: her pearl necklace! "How did you get that? You give me my pearls back right now!" she yelled, and reached her hand out to snatch them.

The shark shook its head and opened its mouth again. In one huge rush, it zoomed toward Pearl.

"Help! Help!" Pearl screamed, and lunged sideways.

The ocean was a blur as she dashed back to Trident Academy as fast as she could. The shark chased Pearl, snapping at her tail.

Pearl didn't have time to think. When she finally burst into the school, she paused to catch her breath. Surely she'd be safe in Trident Academy.

But the shark *didn't* stop. It burst into the tremendous shell and came dangerously close to Pearl.

"Someone! Anyone! Help!" Pearl screamed into the massive empty entrance hall. But no one heard her cries. Everyone at Trident Academy was still in the cafeteria, eating lunch.

Pearl kept racing away from the shark, toward the girls' dormitory.

She was swimming into a dead end, but she had no choice.

Trapped

PEARL ZOOMED DOWN THE hallway. She was trapped, but safe. *He'll never fit here*, she thought. She had to figure out how to warn the school. After all, lunch would be over soon and the rest of the merstudents would be swimming into danger. For once Pearl

actually wished the Shark Guard was with her.

A huge *swoosh* of water knocked her to the bottom of the shell. *Oh no!* The shark had followed her into the dorm! One of its fins was trapped in a seaweed curtain, or it would have surely eaten her. The shark jerked violently back and forth, with Pearl's necklace dangling from its mouth.

Pearl desperately backed away. "Mrs. Karp! Headmaster Hermit!" she squeaked. She was barely able to get the words out.

Just as the shark broke free, she felt a hand on her back!

"Pearl! Get in here!" Kiki whispered, pulling her into the killer whale skeleton. Shelly, Echo, and Wanda were already huddled inside. The girls had tilted it so that the ribs protected them from the great white.

"You saved me," Pearl said to Kiki.

Kiki shook her head. "We're not out of the fishbowl yet."

The shark headed right at them, its mouth open wide. Pearl whined, "Where's my mother?" But the shark stopped short when it saw the skeleton.

"Pearl, does that shark have a *necklace* in its mouth?" Echo asked.

"Yes. My pearls!" said Pearl. "Kiki, I'm sorry I said you took them."

Shelly gasped. "I can't believe a shark got your necklace."

"Neither can I," Pearl said. "But we're trapped. We have to make a dash for it."

"I'm not leaving this skeleton," Echo said. "For just this once I feel safe inside a killer whale!"

"I'd rather be inside this killer whale than that shark!" Shelly said while the great white sniffed the skeleton.

Kiki held Pearl back. "Don't, Pearl. We have to stay right where we are."

"But we don't have to be quiet about it," Pearl replied.

"Help!" they all yelled as the shark

banged the skeleton with its snout. The girls clutched one another.

"We're not loud enough," Pearl said. "We're doomed!"

"Too bad we don't have one of those human things Grandfather Siren told me about. It makes voices louder," Echo said.

Pearl's green eyes widened. "Echo, you just gave me the greatest idea. Shelly, remember how you sang at my birthday a few weeks ago? Sing your loudest. Just like you did at my party," Pearl said. She had been mad at Shelly for singing so well, but now they needed someone whose voice could be heard.

Shelly didn't waste a second. She tilted

her head back and sang in her loudest, highest voice, "HEEEELLLLLLPPPPPPP!"

"Surely someone heard that," Wanda said.

"I hope so," Pearl answered. "It might be our last chance."

10

Surprise

SUDDENLY, A DARK SHADOW loomed in the hallway.

"Oh no!" Pearl squealed. "Is that *another* shark?" Great whites usually traveled alone, and one was more than enough to worry about. Two was beyond horrible.

The great white shark kept pushing and shoving the skeleton with its snout, turning it upside down. Sharp teeth snapped toward Pearl. Closing her eyes, she braced herself. But . . .

Nothing happened! Instead, she heard a loud *SLAP!*

Pearl opened her eyes and saw the great white sliding backward out of the dorm. The girls didn't move a fin or take a breath. But the shark didn't return.

Finally Shelly found her voice. "What just happened?"

"The shark left," Kiki whispered.

"But why?" Echo asked.

Pearl peered out of the skeleton. She

jumped backward when a shadowy figure appeared. But it wasn't a shark.

"Mr. *Fangtooth*!" Pearl said in shock. She couldn't believe her eyes.

"Yes, Pearl, it's me," Mr. Fangtooth said in his grumpy voice.

"Be careful," Echo warned. "There are sharks out there!"

Mr. Fangtooth swam over to Kiki's killer whale skeleton bed. "Not anymore, girls," he said. "I chased it away. There was only one. A big one, but only one."

Pearl's mouth popped open in surprise. "*You* got rid of it?"

Mr. Fangtooth smiled, showing a huge fanglike front tooth. "He's gone. After all,

I used to be a colonel in the Shark Patrol before I retired. Didn't your guard tell you? He's my nephew."

"He is? You were?" Pearl asked with newfound respect for Mr. Fangtooth. Now she was sorry for the mean faces she had once made at him.

"Lucky for you ladies, my tail is ultra-sensitive and it tingles whenever there's a great white around," Mr. Fangtooth explained. "The rest of Trident Academy is in lockdown in the cafeteria."

"And I do have to thank Shelly," he continued. "Her singing helped me find you faster."

The girls rushed out of the skeleton and gathered around Mr. Fangtooth.

"Thank you so much," they said.

Even Pearl nodded. "You saved our lives."

"All in a day's work," Mr. Fangtooth said, and started to swim away. Then he stopped. "Oh, I believe this belongs to you." He handed Pearl her long, gleaming, white pearl necklace.

"My pearls! Thank you, Mr. Fangtooth," she said. "These belonged to my grand-mother."

Kiki swam to Pearl. "No wonder you were so upset when you lost them," she said. "They must be extra-special to you, right?"

Pearl smiled back at her. "Yes, they are. They make me feel close to her when I wear them."

After Mr. Fangtooth left, the mergirls finished moving Kiki's bed into her room. Even Pearl helped.

When they were done, Kiki looked around her new home and at her friends. "I want *all* of you to visit me, okay?" she said. "Now you know this skeleton won't harm you. It even protected us from a great white shark, right?"

"And a new room is always better with friends," Wanda added.

Echo grinned. "What an amazing day," she said, "but we'd better get to class."

Shelly giggled. "I'll tell you what was really amazing," she said.

"What?" Kiki asked.

Shelly grinned. "Pearl is the one who *finally* got Mr. Fangtooth to smile!"

Class Reports

★ ✦ ★

GREAT WHITE SHARK

By Shelly Siren

The great white shark's teeth can be as long as a mergirl's hand. Their teeth have serrated edges that look razor sharp. They are able to rip through the toughest flesh. Luckily for us at Trident Academy, we have a retired colonel from the Shark Patrol, Mr. Fangtooth, working right here at our school to protect us.

CHAIN CATSHARK

By Echo Reef

This funny-looking shark is the only kind I hope I ever see. Its body is covered with what looks like chains from an ancient sailing ship. I like it because it only eats worms, crustaceans, and small fish.

FRILLED SHARK

By Rocky Ridge

My dad wouldn't let me turn in a report on the bloodiest of all sharks, the great white. What a bummer that I didn't get to see the one that came inside Trident Academy. That would have been totally cool. I had to do my second-favorite shark, the frilled shark. I like it because it always has this weird-looking smile on its face. Each of its huge teeth has three sharp points. The frilled shark doesn't even look like a shark. It looks like an eel and eats little fish and squid.

TASSELED WOBBEGONG

By Pearl Swamp

All sharks are horrible, disgusting creatures. The tasseled wobbegong is not only a shark, but it also is the weirdest-looking shark. Once my dad was swimming along the ocean floor in the evening, and a tasseled wobbegong reached up and tried to eat my dad's tail! My dad still has the scars to prove it. My dad didn't even see the shark because it looks like the ocean floor!

BLUE SHARK

By Kiki Coral

I chose to write about the blue shark because I think it is the prettiest of all sharks. I like its beautiful blue color and its dark eyes rimmed with white. It is also an ocean wanderer, like me. This shark is very fast and can outswim most merfolk. Luckily, it doesn't usually bother merpeople or humans, although it has on occasion. Its numbers are declining because humans have killed them for sport or food.

The Mermaid Song

REFRAIN:

Let the water roar

Deep down we're swimming along

Twirling, swirling, singing the mermaid song.

VERSE 1:

Shelly flips her tail

Racing, diving, chasing a whale

Twirling, swirling, singing the mermaid song.

VERSE 2:

Pearl likes to shine

Oh my Neptune, she looks so fine

Twirling, swirling, singing the mermaid song.

VERSE 3:

Shining Echo flips her tail

Backward and forward without fail

Twirling, swirling, singing the mermaid song.

VERSE 4:

Amazing Kiki

Far from home and floating so free

Twirling, swirling, singing the mermaid song.

Author's Note

I AM VERY EXCITED TO BE GOING TO visit the ocean very soon. I am hoping to see lots of interesting creatures, but there is one I definitely do not wish to see—a great white! I do want to see a mermaid! Check out the Mermaid Tales section of www.debbiedadey.com to learn how to make your own mermaid club and to find out which kind of mermaid you are! I hope you'll keep reading the next few pages for more information on the fascinating creatures mentioned in *Danger in the Deep Blue Sea.*

Dive into reading,
Debbie Dadey

Glossary

BLACK-LIP OYSTER: This oyster lives in the Gulf of Mexico, in the western Pacific Ocean, and in the western and eastern Indian Ocean.

CLAM: Creatures called mollusks live inside shells, like clams and oysters. The biggest and heaviest of the mollusks (there are over fifty thousand types of them) is the giant clam.

CORAL: Carnation coral is the most colorful of reef animals. They can be red, pink, orange, white, or yellow.

COWRIE: The flamingo tongue cowrie has an off-white shell that is usually hidden by two leopard-spotted extensions.

CRAB: When the blue swimming crab feels scared, it buries itself in the sand.

DOLPHIN: Dolphins love to travel in groups. The spinner dolphin will swim in groups of up to several thousand.

GRAY HERON: The gray heron is a tall, long-legged bird that feeds on fish.

GRAY LICHEN: The gray lichen forms little blackish-brown patches on rocks or shells.

HAGFISH: The Pacific hagfish lives in the mud, and it usually survives by eating dead fish.

JELLYFISH: The mauve stinger jellyfish makes a glowing light show, but its sting hurts!

KELP: Off the coast of California is a bed of giant kelp, the biggest of all seaweeds. Sea otters live in the kelp forest.

KILLER WHALE: The killer whale, or orca, is the largest member of the dolphin family.

LONGHORN COWFISH: This fish has very long fleshy horns above its eyes.

MOTHER-OF-PEARL: This is a shiny layer inside some oyster shells. In the past, it was often used for making beautiful buttons.

OYSTERS: Creatures called mollusks live inside shells. Some mollusks have the ability to create pearls and are called feathered oysters. One type of feathered oyster is the Shark's Bay pearl oyster.

PLANKTON: Plankton are tiny animals that drift with the ocean currents and live in the surface section of the ocean.

RED LIONFISH: This night-loving fish has poison glands on its dorsal fin.

SABLEFISH: Sablefish numbers have declined rapidly because they are slow breeders. It takes fourteen years to replace each fish caught!

SEA HORSE: The male sea horse stores the eggs until they are ready to hatch!

SEAWEED: There are many types of seaweed. The small jelly weed is used in making jam and preserving meat and fish. It's even used in science experiments.

SHARKS

- **BLUE SHARK:** This long (thirteen feet) blue shark crosses the ocean looking for food.

- **CHAIN CATSHARK:** This shark has cat-like eyes and strange markings covering its body, making it look like it is wearing chains.

- **FRILLED SHARK:** This shark doesn't look like a shark at all, but it does look happy. The eel-like creature often swims with its mouth open, showing large white teeth like it is smiling.

- **GREAT WHITE:** This 3.7-ton shark can be twenty-four feet long.

- **TASSELED WOBBEGONG:** This shark

manages to look just like a seaweed-covered rock.

SWORDFISH: This fish gets its name from its long, sword-like snout.

WHALE: Beluga whales were once called the "canaries of the sea" because their sounds could be heard through the hulls of wooden sailing ships. Today their numbers are greatly reduced because they have been hunted and they are hurt by pollution and shipping traffic.

Debbie Dadey

is the author and coauthor of one hundred and fifty children's books, including the series The Adventures of the Bailey School Kids. A former teacher and librarian, Debbie now lives in Bucks County, Pennsylvania, with her wonderful husband and children. They live about two hours from the ocean and love to go there to look for mermaids. If you see any, let her know at www.debbiedadey.com.

Trouble at Trident Academy

Battle of the Best Friends

A Whale of a Tale

Danger in the Deep Blue Sea

COLLECT THEM ALL!

The Lost Princess

The Secret Sea Horse

Dream of the Blue Turtle

Treasure in Trident City